February 5, 1987

Enjoy Willo Mancifoot!
Love,
Valerie

Willo Mancifoot

and the Mugga Killa Whomps

Written and illustrated by

Valerie Hubbard Damon

Star Publications ★ Kansas City, Missouri

National Publication Date April 2, 1985

International Children's Book Day

Copyright ©1985 by Star Publications

Library of Congress Number 83-050739
ISBN 0-932356-07-9
ISBN 0-932356-08-7 Limited Art Edition

FIRST EDITION

ALL
★ Rights Reserved ★

Published by

Star Publications
1211 West 60th Terrace
Kansas City, Missouri 64113

2 - 87

Printed and bound in the United States of America

This book is printed with a 200-line screen
on heavy acid-free paper.

★   ★

In memory of
Richard James Hubbard,
my dear father.

Now come with me to Willobee,
A land both small and grand.
Come down on your knees
Below root trees,
Softly across the sand.
There you can see by a mushroom tree
A village of strange creations,
With fright things, Light Wings
And fly-in-the-night things
Partaking in grand celebration.

We dance every night
By Light Wing light
With food and drinks so fine,
Made from the fragrant flowers
Of beautiful sweet Flame Vine.
"Life is good,
Sweet harmony grows,
Our friends are here,
Tomorrow may go . . .

"So come, tip a cup
Of nectar with me
And join in a dance
On Spirillus Fungee!
Fungee Fungee Fungee hee hee!
Come join in a dance
On Spirillus Fungee!"

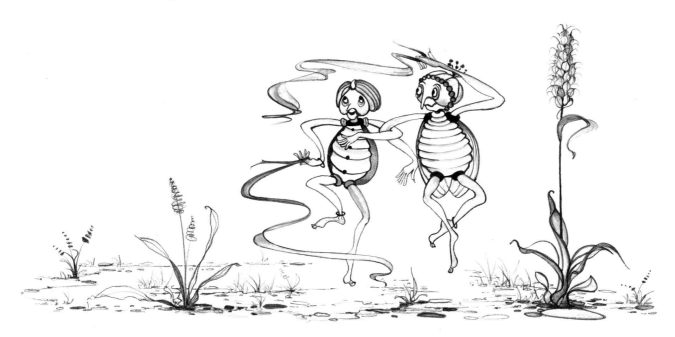

Dawn has come,
There's work to be done;
All stretch and yawn
In their nests.
The first to arise
Collect their supplies
And do what they do best.
Their chores in time
Lead to Flame Vine
Where they tend and water her roots.
And in this way
Food for their days
Begins with tiny pink shoots.

Prayer for Flame Vine

"Flame Vine, entwine your design for me;
Food for **Light Wings** comes from thee.
Flame Vine, give your gift of life:
Light Wings **feed** and **glow** at night.
Nectar and the golden pollen
Is food for precious life for all,
And you must know we love you so:
Thank you, dear Flame Vine."

Hortet Corbet Light Wings Micket Wee Cricket Willo Mancifoot Flame Vine

Hortet Corbet is a great gourmet.
The Pollen Star Tarts
She bakes every day
Are quite a sight,
A real delight
For friends in Willobee Land.

Micket Wee Cricket holds in his hand
A feeder he made and placed in the sand
To light the nights in Willobee Land
And shine on golden paths.
What a sensation,
His feeder creations
Glowing bright in the night,
Where Light Wings feed
On the pollen they need
To live and glow brilliant light.
Micket loved tarts
With his Wee Cricket heart
And especially his Wee Cricket tongue;
He would chat and trade
The feeders he made
For tarts, and savor each crumb.

Willo Mancifoot, Willo Mancifoot,
Giant Wings and dapper green look,
A kindly dragon who carefully took
Great care of the dear Flame Vines.
The pollen and nectar he gathered each day
Were traded for tarts with the great gourmet.
Their balance in life provided the way
For peace and harmony.

And so it was, because because
They all loved tarts
They all were found
Quite often together
In all sorts of weather
At dear Hortet's, gathered round
A table of food
And mugs of herb tea—
A festively breakfasty feast.
They would chat and trade
The products they made
And eat and eat and eat:

Far away past the bottomless deep
In the Swamp of Ornay
Where the Mug Roots creep
Is a very different place
Where gruff and grumpy faces
Are peeping out of spaces
From the dark and decay.
They are Mugga Killa Whomps
And they whomp and they stomp
And they grumble and they stumble.
They are not too bright!
All was dismal in their lives,
Misty dark and lightless nights,
Resulting in the plight
Of Triagondal Blue:
He tripped on a root
And spilled his tea.
He broke his cup
And skinned his knee.
He stomped and yelled
"I want to see.

"If I had **light**
Then I'd be **free**
From stumbling, bumbling nights.
It's such a dismal plight!
Now gather round, my fellow whompers.
I will choose two mighty stompers!
I must have light.
Not one more night
Will I fight
In dark and confusion.
Listen to me
My plan will take three.
I think I have the solution.
I've heard of a place
By a mushroom base
Where Light Wings live and **glow**.
We'll stomp them and then
We'll whomp them and then
We'll grab three Wings and go!
Might makes right and we need light!
Might makes right and we need light!"

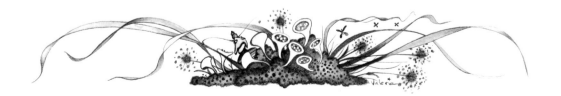

Two of the mightiest Killa Whomps
Known to all as Clomp and Stomp
Came running and yelling,
"Me want, me want,
We want to go."
Triagondal Blue said, "Follow me.
We'll gather hooking thorns, then we
Will make strong cages.
We'll need just three.
Then we'll chop and stomp
Our way through the swamp.
We'll cross the Bottomless Deep,
Stomp through the forest of green.
We'll search each part of the sky
Until glowing wings are seen."

The trio was off,
With no way of knowing
What lay ahead
Or where they were going.
Clomp and Stomp complained
And were groaning,
"I can't see the sky,
No light is showing."
They came to the Bottomless Deep,
Heard the howling winds below.
They stomped through the forest of green
Where the sky began to show:
"A glow! A glow!
Could it be?
Light Wing glow
By a Mushroom Tree?"
They ran off in the night
Full of excitement:
"Might makes right.
And we want light!"

The Mugga Killa Whomps were right.
There they saw a wondrous sight:
Glowing wings of brilliant light,
And then they said,
"I am Clomp and I am Stomp.
We are Mugga Killa Whomps.
We are very good at whomping.
We **want** you.
You see your light;
Your wondrous light
Will nicely brighten up our night.
You know that might is always right,
And we've **got** you!"
The smallest Light Wing barely escaped,
Injured his foot, then flew to a safe
Place on gold sand
In Willobee Land
Where he hid in the ferns for awhile.

The Mighty Mugga Killa Whomps
Ran off toward the dismal Swamp of Ornay,
Where stink and decay
Are all around and hug the ground.
The only sound was way down the path.
Through the plants came a chanting
As the panting, panting, panting,
Killa Whomps sang their song:
"We are mighty Killa Whompers.
We are mighty whomp and stompers.
You know might is always right
And we whomped you!"

Their camp was full of screaming.
When they reached it there were teeming
Killa Whompers who came streaming
To the light, **fading** light.
They began a stomping scene:
It was like a horrid dream
Eating berries by their green
Precious light, **fading** light.

In the middle of Willobee Land
The wounded Light Wing fluttered to land
On the mushroom Spirillus Fungee
Where all his friends came quickly to see:
Micket brought his healing herbs,
Mancifoot spoke calming words.
Then the Light Wing cried,
"There were three Killa Whomps . . .
Left a trail to the swamp . . .
With a whomp and a stomp,
They took three Light Wings.
I was wounded when I fled.
Oh my leg is very red
On my hinged foot-a-ped!
Ohhhhhhhhhh!"

Willo Mancifoot thought of a rescue plan.
He was very wise.
Then the kindly dragon said,
Looking toward the sky,
"To have great power in Killa Whomp eyes,
We must use the element of surprise.
And with a grandiose costume disguise,
They'll freeze in fear for their
Killa Whomp lives!

I can be a glowing dragon—
A grand fire-breathing dragon—
Gather pollen in a wagon
For my wings to glow.
The Mugga Killa Whomps want light,
But first they need a vine.
We'll show them how to grow a seed
Then tell them how to find
The value of cooperation,
The balance and the fine relation
To a vine and its creation
Of the Light Wing's light."

Micket said, "Quite so!
That will work, don't you know?
And I see such a sight
In my own mind's eye.
I will sketch upon the sand
Supplies we need to have on hand
As we devise this dragon plan
To save our friends.

Together we can be a team;
We'll all glue pollen on your wings.
Then I will come so I can bring
The Flame Vine Seed."

We shall use a flower
For the dragon mask.
Gather cups of nectar
For the other task
Of gluing and securing
All the pollen dust.
Finish it by twilight,
Yes we must, must, must!
Light Wings, paint nectar
On the dragon wings.
Hortet, plan the headdress
As you help to bring
The greenleaves and the grasses
From the golden sand.
Now everyone start working
On the dragon plan."

Grass tips glued on Willo's fingers
Made his claws a fearsome sight.
A beaded dust pouch on his shoulder
Held the glowing pollen right
Beside where he could put it
In his mouth so he might blow
A dragon flame of glowing pollen
So all the Killa Whomps would know
The mighty dragon of Willobee Land
All scaly green and very grand.
His mighty flame makes everyone look!
And his name is Willo Mancifoot!

Down the great mountain
Of green they flew.
The end of the trail
Was seen, and who
Would have thought it could be?
There was no way to see
Where the Whompers had taken
The three Light Wings.

Only a tunnel through plants was there,
Too small for the dragon.
" I can't," he declared,
"See a way we can do it!
We can not fit through it!"
Then they wept by the Bottomless Deep
In despair.
Tears of pain,
Tears of loss
So much the same
All hope seemed lost.

Down below in the Bottomless Deep
A magic wind through rocks did creep
And softly it began to sing
A rhyme for dragon ears:

"A real dragon's might
Depends on **his** sight
To see what **you** might know.
The lines in the grass,
Each one as you pass
Holds many secrets and shows
Where Whompers are dwelling
And clearly is telling
The place where Light Wings glow.
See what there is:
The grass tells the secret to all.
Let your mind growww."

They looked upon the growing plants,
Stopped thinking thoughts of
"No, we can't,"
Then noticed a peculiar slant.
Then Willo cried, "I know!
I know! I know! I see the sign!
Now I understand the rhyme.
The plants knew it all the time.
Our lives each day create a kind
Of path, and now the plants
Will help us find our way."

"The grass, the grass
Tells **all** as we pass.
The lines define our path all the way.
Have faith in your feelings
In forest floor ceilings.
Take care, with care
The positive way."

Above the swamp the dragon flew;
The plants and grass were pointing to
Some gnarled roots all grayish blue
And Light Wing Light!
The camp of Mugga Killa Whomps
In the Mug Roots, in the Swamp
Was filled with brilliant dragon light.
The dragon's flame caused frightened
Killa Whomps to bow their heads.
And then the mighty dragon said,
"Your stomping days and brutish ways
Must end if you want light.
Stop thinking ME and learn to SEE
And simply do what's right!
The more you give, the more you have;
Now give to one another.
Cooperate in harmony
And learn to love your brother.

"Together plant this vine seed.
I'll help you choose the site.
Be good to it and kind to it
And when the time is right,
Flowers bloom, Light Wings come
To drink and share their light.
You both will share the bounty there,
The food and glow at night.
But in a cage Light Wings fade
And will die a silent death!
Now free my friends and I will send
A seed from magic dragon's breath.
I'll bless the ground, come gather round,
This spot will do just fine.
Tend it well and learn to love
The life within a vine."
From the dragon's breath of fire
A Flame Vine seed fell to the ground.
Great fear and terror filled their hearts,
No Killa Whomp could make a sound.

Triagondal Blue, who wanted the light,
Quickly set the Light Wings free.
He mumbled and stammered
And tried to explain,
Then said, "Whompers, listen to me.
Now the time has come for change.
Today we start to rearrange
Our lives if we want light.
I'm older and my stomping days
Seem foolish, and this better way
Could make a happy life."

"But might makes right,
And we want light,"
Said all the Mugga Killa Whomps.

"Might makes fights
And leaves our nights
A dismal plight
When Light Wings die.
I'm sure in time
Our hearts could find
Love for a vine
If we just try."

"Perhaps it's true, we'll follow you.
We'll see if vines can bring
Glowing light into our nights?
We haven't lost a thing!
But still it's strange to rearrange
Our stomping brutish ways.
For a vine? Perhaps in time.
It could take many days!"

The dragon left
With flaming breath.
And vanished in the Swamp.
Now came the days
Of changing ways
For Mugga Killa Whomps.

Change for Light
Light for Change
MKW

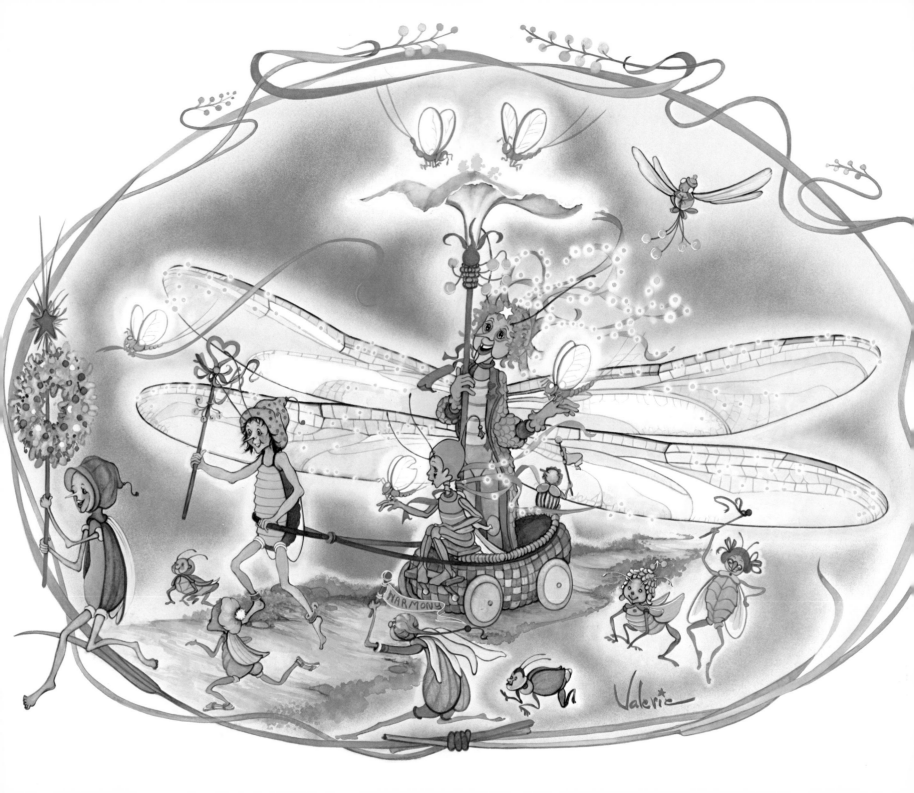

Every creature in Willobee Land
Was waiting there on golden sand,
Hoping that the dragon's plan
Would turn out right.
First a glowing light was seen,
Then the dragon's brilliant wings
Flew and landed in between
The Mushroom Trees.

Sweet nectar for the Light Wings!
A cheer for the dragon!
Hurray for the plants!
Parade in the wagon!
They removed the dragon tail
As festive bells began to ring.
They danced upon the golden paths.
And everyone began to sing:
"Take me away on your dragonfly wings.
Play a note for me. Let it ring, ring, ring.
You know my heart's true and my trust is there,
And I will follow you anywhere.
So take me away on your dragonfly wings.
Giving helpful seeds makes me sing, sing, sing.
Tomorrow's adventures become our new songs.
Play a note for me and I'll sing along."

FLAME VINE SEEDS

Epilogue of Willobee Land

And so it continued in Willobee Land,
A beautiful life on golden sand.
On fine windy days sweet songs were heard
From Bottomless Deep, sharing new words.
And all would learn the truthful songs
Of love and peace and sing along.

Love and harmony. Peace and truth.

Of all the Mugga Killa Whomps
In the Mug Roots, in the Swamp
Triagondal Blue was first to change.
He really worked to rearrange
His life for a vine and Light Wing light.
And soon, his example became the brightest
Light, true light!

Change for light. Light for change.